BABOON

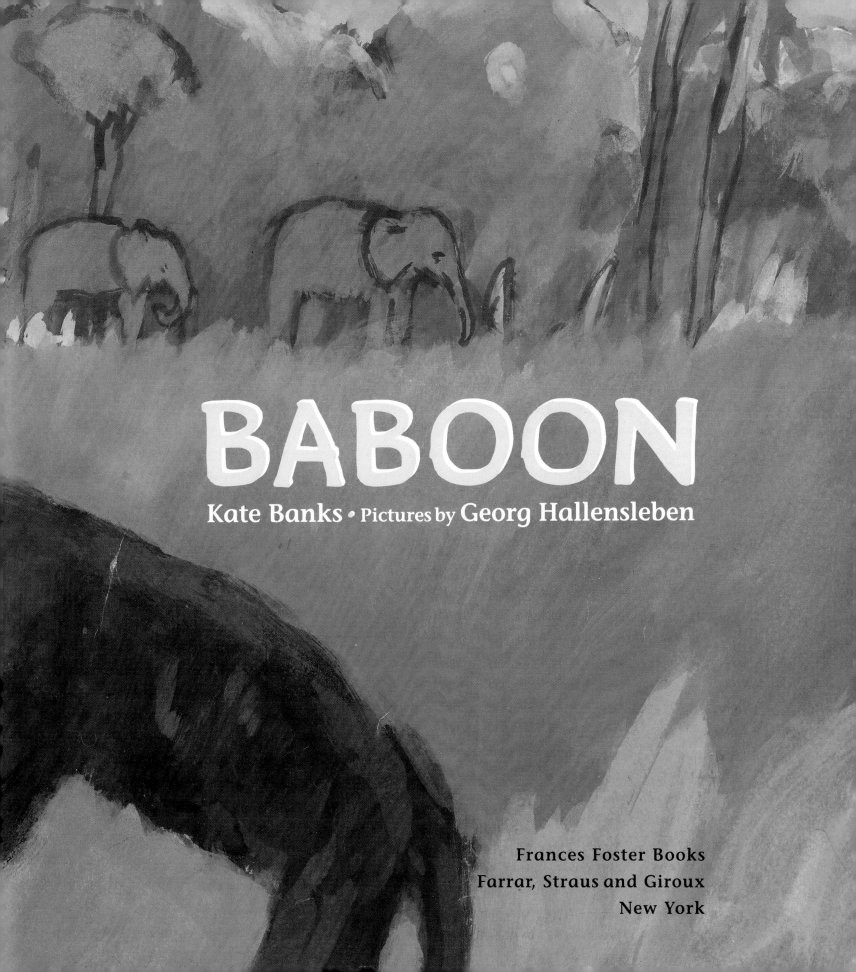

BABOON

Kate Banks • Pictures by Georg Hallensleben

Frances Foster Books
Farrar, Straus and Giroux
New York

Baboon opened his sleepy eyes.
Ahead was the great forest.
"Look," said his mother. "That is
the world."
Baboon slid from his mother's back.
"So, the world is green," he said.
"Some of it," said his mother. And
she led Baboon among the tall trees.

A turtle sat in the middle of the road.
Its eyes were closed and it barely moved.
Baboon watched and waited for the turtle
to pass. He waited a long time.
"The world is slow," he said.
"It can be," said his mother.

When the turtle had passed, Baboon followed
his mother.
At the edge of the great forest, a fire burned
in the bush.
Baboon moved close to the fire.
Soon he could feel its heat.
Baboon leaped backward.
"The world is hot!" he said.
"Not always," said his mother.

She led Baboon to a small lake.
A crocodile lay on the sandy bank.
It opened its mouth wide.
"Careful," said Baboon's mother.
"The crocodile might eat you."
Baboon did not want to be eaten.
So he ran into the bush.
"The world is hungry," he said.
"Sometimes you are hungry, too,"
said his mother.

Soon the elephants came, four by four.
They thundered loud and shook the ground.
A gazelle passed. He was not slow like the
turtle, but quick and fast.

A rhinoceros darted out of the bushes.
He grunted at Baboon. Baboon was afraid.
"He will not hurt you," said his mother.

Baboon took his mother's hand, and they started across a field.

Baboon hid in the tall grass.

His mother hid, too. When they found each other, they lay down, side by side.

"The world is soft," said Baboon. And he was happy.

Baboon stretched and rolled over.
A bird flew by. A cloud passed
overhead. And Baboon fell asleep.
When he awoke, the sun was going down.
Baboon watched it disappear behind the trees.
"Come along," said his mother. And they
walked on.

Baboon followed his mother up
a tree.
Across from him sat a monkey.
He was like Baboon.
"Is he the world, too?" asked Baboon.
"He is," said his mother. "Just as
you are."
Baboon watched quietly.
Then he followed his mother down
the tree.

Now the elephants were huddled together. The
gazelles were resting.
There was no more fire and the light was gone
from the sky.
Baboon climbed onto his mother's back.
"The world is dark," he said.
"Sometimes," whispered his mother, carrying
him home.

Baboon looked around.

He blinked.

Everything was black as far as he could see.

He laid his head against his mother's soft neck.

"The world is big," he said.

"Yes," said his mother softly. "The world is big."

Text copyright © 1997 by Kate Banks
Pictures copyright © 1997 by Georg Hallensleben
Originally published in French under the title *Baboon*,
copyright © 1994 by Editions Gallimard
All rights reserved
Published simultaneously in Canada by HarperCollins*CanadaLtd*
Printed in Italy
Designed by Caitlin Martin
First American edition, 1997

Library of Congress Cataloging-in-Publication Data
Banks, Kate.
Baboon / Kate Banks ; pictures by Georg Hallensleben. — 1st ed.
p.   cm.
"Frances Foster books."
Summary: A young baboon's view of the world changes as his mother
shows him various parts of his environment.
ISBN 0-374-30474-2
[1. Baboons—Fiction. 2. Animals—Fiction. 3. Perception—Ficiton.]
I. Hallensleben, George, ill. II. Title.
PZ7.B22594Bab   1997
[E]—dc20   96-20888   CIP   AC